A Fish Who Had A Wish

Daniel Silverhawk

To order additional copies of this book, contact:
Xlibris
844-714-8691
www.Xlibris.com
Orders@Xlibris.com

ISBN: Softcover   978-1-6698-2178-6
       Hardcover   978-1-6698-7236-8
       EBook   978-1-6698-2179-3
Library of Congress Control Number: 2023905926

Print information available on the last page

Rev. date: 03/28/2023

A FISH WHO HAD A WISH

Acknowledgements:

Special thanks to all my friends like my dear friend, Olivia Revier who masterfully illustrated this book. <u>*ovrevier@gmail.com*</u>

More books by Daniel Silverhawk:

The Puppy in Disguise
Petunia's Garden
The Old Pond Slums

Once upon a time
there was a little guppy fish;
Who lived out in the ocean blue,
and had a great big wish!

The guppy wanted to share his wish,
while making friends and building bonds;
So he used his shell-phone to call some friends,
living in basins, lakes, and ponds.

He wished that he could make his wish come true
by searching the sand and coral reef.
He knew his wish must come true somehow,
and he held on to that belief.

He did not know what to say or do,
and he didn't know what to try,
So he wished upon a starfish, fish;
but the starfish asked him why.

"Why did you wish your wish on me?"
"Your wish I can not grant."
"I wish I could make your
wish come true,"
"I want to, but I can't."

"You should ask the 'Big Blue Whale'
down at the southern tip,"
"He lives down on the ocean floor,
inside a sunken ship."

So the guppy left to find the whale
along the ocean floor.
To ask the whale to grant his wish,
"That's all I'm asking for."

He swam up to the sunken ship
and found an opening in the top;
But a giant squid named, 'The Ink Blot Kid,'
had ordered him to "Stop!"

"The big blue whale is a busy whale,
and busy whales must eat!"
So, he brought the guppy to a waiting room
and had him take a seat.

The guppy waited patiently
for the whale to eat his krill,
then he told the whale all about his wish,
and how it somehow must be real.

The big blue whale thought earnestly,
as he surfaced to blow some air;
But the big blue whale didn't have a wish;
There were no wishes made down there.

And since the whale had never made a wish,
he simply had no clue;
So he said, "You should try the Northern Sea."
And that was all he said to do.

Now, the guppy was willing to go the extra mile,
and to do whatever it takes.
He searched the wetlands and
through the swamps.
He talked to the alligators, and eels, and snakes.

The guppy listened to
a babbling brook,
while he floated down
a gentle stream.
He took a nap in a river bed,
And his wish became a dream.

The further North the guppy swam,
and the bigger the guppy grew;
The more determined he did become,
and the bigger his wish grew too.

He swam with some
salmon to a mountaintop,
while searching the
rocks along the way;
And he swam for a while
with a school of fish,
but he didn't have
time to play.

He swam through ice and tidal waves,
he swam through wind and rain.
He swam through hail and thunderstorms,
and through a hurricane.

The guppy swam to the far North Pole,
in search of someone wise.
He swam up to an otter's den,
to ask the 'Otter Guys.'

"We cannot grant your wish my friend,
but we're so happy that you came."
"Because every fish has a different wish,
but they are wishes just the same."

The otters called a conference
to discuss the guppy's need;
"The guppy needs the otter's help,"
"They must find help indeed!"

The otters called the octopus,
who called the great white shark;
The shark then called the polar bears,
who said it must be dark.

"The ocean floor is dark, that's true,
but the stars are in the sky."
"You must go where the sky is dark,
that's what you need to try."

The guppy thanked the otters and swam away,
on the surface of the sea.
He swam in search of the setting sun;
That's where his wish must be!

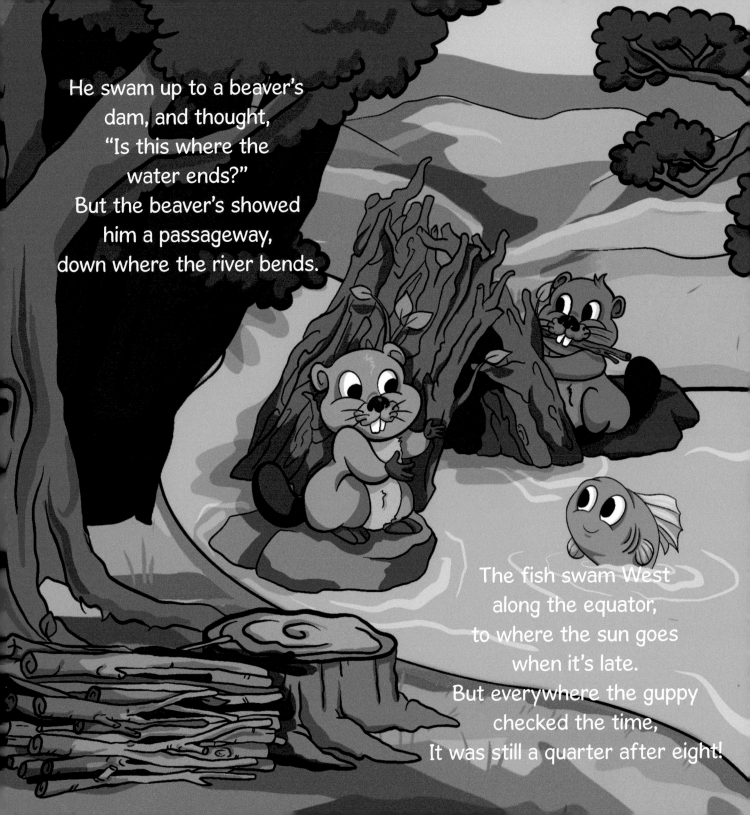

He swam up to a beaver's
dam, and thought,
"Is this where the
water ends?"
But the beaver's showed
him a passageway,
down where the river bends.

The fish swam West
along the equator,
to where the sun goes
when it's late.
But everywhere the guppy
checked the time,
It was still a quarter after eight!

"I do not know or understand
why the sun won't disappear,"
"I swam around the world to find
the sun was shining there."

He asked a stingray, "What went wrong?"
"I did as I was told."
The stingray checked his database,
And he checked his watch of gold;

He checked the diameter of the earth,
and the sun up in the sky;
He watched the shadow that his fins had made,
and found the reason why:

You can tell your wish to the first star you see.
You don't have to wait for one to fall.
Then follow your dream like you believe in it,
And it may come true after all!

So, the guppy turned back to the East
and as he waved to say goodbye,
He was sure to get his wish this time,
and here's the reason why...

In the East, in the dark of night,
when he closed his little eyes;
He made a wish on the first star he saw,
only then to realize...

The guppy's wish was to see the world,
and he saw the whole world wide.
While he kept on searching for his wish,
and wouldn't let it stay inside.

And he wished that he would make new friends,
As he shared his wish along the way
And he made new friends over a common goal:
To see a wish come true that day!

And he wished that all the friends he made
had wishes that all came true.
Now, all his friends are making wishes,
-And you can make one too!

Keep on searching for your wish, my friend.
And share every goal that you accomplish,
All your friends will have dreams to follow,
like the "Fish Who had a Wish!"

the beginning...

Printed in the United States
by Baker & Taylor Publisher Services